Meet the Stars of

7th Heaven

The Only Unofficial Scrapbook

by Matt Netter

SCHOLASTIC INC.
New York Toronto London Auckland Sydney
Mexico City New Delhi Hong Kong

Photo Credits

dedication

To my parents, who filled my childhood with love and joy, and my big brother, who made sure nobody picked on me.

about the author

Matt Netter is a freelance writer working and living in New York City. He is also the author of several other young reader entertainment books, including *The New York Times* **best-seller** *Zac Hanson: Totally Zac.* **He's currently at work on a fictional Christmas story, loosely based on his childhood.**

ISBN 0-439-04299-2

12 11 10 9 8 7 6 5 4 3 2 1   9/9 0 1 2 3 4/0

Book Design by Dawn Adelman

Printed in the U.S.A.
First Scholastic printing, February 1999

Introduction

Every Monday evening millions of loyal *7th Heaven* fans are invited over to dinner with the warmest family in America, the Camdens. At one end of the table sits the Reverend Eric Camden, devoted husband, father, and community leader. Mrs. Annie Camden, mother, homemaker, and, without question, the glue of the family, sits opposite her husband at the other end. In between are their five children and, in dual infant seats, the new babies.

Matt, the oldest, is 17. He's grown from a long-haired, rebellious teen into a responsible young adult — most of the time, that is. He sits next to athletic Mary, who goes to high school and is still trying to figure out boys, friends, and everything else. Blond-haired 11-year-old Simon is adorable and sharp, but relentless in his pursuit of what he wants. He sits next to Lucy, who's two years his elder, but very confused about how she should act and dress, and where she fits in. Ruthie, 6, is a little curly-haired dynamo who's usually vying for everyone's attention.

Lately, more and more people are joining the Camdens at that table. *7th Heaven* is currently the number one show among teenagers.

Here's how it all began.

The Backstory

Before the fall of 1996, there were very few wholesome, family-friendly shows on the air, and fewer still revolved around nuclear families (*Home Improvement* was one of the few exceptions). With so many hit shows centering on hospitals, courtrooms, police stations, and school yards, there was a glaring need for a series that focused on the living room and the kitchen.

"I wanted to do a show that families enjoy watching — and I think that's what we've done." That was the vision of *7th Heaven* creator and co-executive producer Brenda Hampton — and she's right, that's exactly what *7th Heaven* achieved.

The creators of *7th Heaven*, including TV legend Aaron Spelling, felt this was a chance to prove that a show like this — wholesome but with a realistic edge — could succeed. Still, none of the four established networks — ABC, CBS, FOX, NBC — would go near it. Only the upstart WB network was more than willing; it embraced the show and immediatly picked up *7th Heaven* for a half-season, 13-episode commitment. The show debuted in September 1996.

All in the Family

The cast bonded quickly. "All the kids, we have such a great time together that we feel like a family," Jessica Biel told a WB reporter. "It's like you have your family at home and then you go to work and you have your new brothers and sisters." That off-camera chemistry, along with the creative team behind *7th Heaven*, is what makes the Camden family seem so real.

Critics and audiences alike "bonded" with *7th Heaven* and it was jubilantly renewed.

Building Momentum

As *7th Heaven* entered its second season, TV viewers of all ages found it — and stuck with it. Adults tuned in for an hour of realism and drama and the family discussions that it evoked afterward. Meanwhile, children and teens across America fell in love with a handsome young cast that seemed to grow more talented with every episode. As Matt, Mary, Lucy, Simon, and Ruthie grew up, so did the actors who played them.

By the end of its second season, *7th Heaven* was the WB's second-highest rated show, behind *Dawson's Creek*, but ahead of *Buffy the Vampire Slayer*. During the following summer hiatus, the WB network decided to make the show even more available to fans by airing repeats of *7th Heaven* on Sunday nights in addition to original episodes on Mondays.

So, hurry up and pull up a seat. There's always room for guests at the Camden house. Your helping of *7th Heaven* — complete with cast biographies, photos, a peek behind the scenes, Web sites, and a few surprises — is now being served.

Barry Watson as Matt Camden

Matt is perhaps the most complex character on *7th Heaven*. As a typical 17-year-old, he strives for balance in a life that includes strict parents, younger siblings, peer pressure, dating, school, and chores. As the oldest in a close-knit family, he often takes on a responsibility far beyond his years. While Matt is definitely cool, in a sense he is a second father in the Camden household.

It's a complex role, and because of that, *7th Heaven*'s producers were very selective in casting the part. The search was over when they screen-tested Barry Watson, a handsome and talented young actor who had previously played a recurring character on the short-lived *Malibu Shores*.

Proof that Barry Watson was perfect came in the way of a fan-mail onslaught at the WB. It didn't take the network long to realize that Barry was a major reason viewers began tuning into *7th Heaven*.

Being Barry

In real life he's the oldest of four siblings, so Barry can certainly relate to his character. "My dad on *7th Heaven* deals with my character the same way my mom did with me when I was growing up," he noted. "She taught me a lot of lessons that I didn't understand until I was older."

"I'm kind of like my character in a sense," Barry explained to *16 Magazine*. "He cares a lot about his family. He truly does. I have a really good, close relationship with my siblings." In fact, despite his busy life as an actor, Barry works at maintaining ties with his family, who now live in Texas and California.

Barry was born on April 23, 1974, in Traverse City, Michigan, and moved to Dallas, Texas, at age eight. Dallas is where it all began. "I was doing some modeling there," Barry explained to *Teen Beat*. "I was young and I thought it was really stupid. I just wanted to be a kid, so I quit." Later on, he turned to acting. "I started auditioning and doing theater and regional commercials," he recalls. "Then I started going to [acting] seminars and classes." He was discovered when a talent agent "came to Dallas, pulled me aside, and asked if I wanted to come to LA. I said, 'Sure!'"

Roll the Credits

Barry's very first acting job? "It was a commercial for Jump Dancer. It was a toy with a spinning thing, like a spinning jump rope. I was just a little guy." Once established in Hollywood, Barry continued to do commercials, and after he graduated from high school, he began to pursue acting in earnest. A number of guest-starring roles followed on TV series like *Baywatch*, *The Nanny*, *Sister, Sister*, and the daytime soap opera *Days of Our Lives*.

Barry took on a couple of TV movies, including *Marina's Story*, and the HBO movie *Attack of the 50-Foot Woman*. His big break was a recurring role as Seth on the Aaron Spelling series *Malibu Shores*.

Trivia alert: While *Malibu Shores* didn't last long, it was a launching pad for a number of young actors. Besides Barry, *Felicity* star Keri Russell, *Buffy the Vampire Slayer*'s Charisma Carpenter, *Sunset Beach*'s Susan Ward, Randy Spelling, and recurring *Melrose Place* star Katie Wright all got their big break on the series.

"Overnight" Sensation

7th Heaven turned Barry into an overnight star and a bona fide teen heartthrob. *YM* tabbed him one of the "50 Most Beautiful Guys in the World" and *Inside Edition* named him one of television's "Hot Hunks of Fall 1996." But Barry takes his fame in stride and opts to devote his energy to being an actor rather than a ham.

In the show's first two seasons Matt matured from rebel without a clue to father-in-training. At the same time Barry blossomed into a breakout TV star and an up-and-coming movie actor. During *7th Heaven*'s 1998 summer hiatus, Barry went on location to film *Killing Mrs. Tingle*. The thriller, directed by *Dawson's Creek* creator and *Scream* writer Kevin Williamson, co-stars Katie Holmes, Vivica A. Fox, and Molly Ringwald, and marks a significant departure from Barry's role on *7th Heaven*. In *Tingle*, Barry plays one of several classmates who kidnap a mean high-school teacher.

According to *YM*, "*7th Heaven* hunk Barry Watson's performance in *Tingle* is gonna turn him into a mega-star."

These days, free time is a rarity for Barry. He takes advantage of what little he has by spending time with his family. His favorite way to relax is to go camping and hiking in the hills with his two dogs, Harsky, his golden retriever–pit bull mix, and his red beagle, Stutch (he's a big fan of the old TV show *Starsky & Hutch*).

So, what's left to know about Barry? He's not married and at last check he didn't have a serious girlfriend. When it comes to dating, there are three things Barry looks for in a girl: intelligence, honesty, and beautiful eyes.

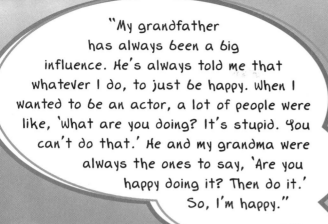

"My grandfather has always been a big influence. He's always told me that whatever I do, to just be happy. When I wanted to be an actor, a lot of people were like, 'What are you doing? It's stupid. You can't do that.' He and my grandma were always the ones to say, 'Are you happy doing it? Then do it.' So, I'm happy."

The Best of Barry

NAME: Barry Watson

DATE OF BIRTH: April 23, 1974

HOMETOWN: Born in Traverse City, Michigan, raised in Dallas, Texas

HEIGHT: 6' 0"

WEIGHT: 170 lbs.

HAIR: Brown

EYES: Hazel

SIBLINGS: Three younger brothers and sisters

PETS: Two dogs, Harsky and Stutch

HOBBIES: Camping and hiking

FUN FACTOID: As a kid, whenever Barry got in trouble, he simply pointed to an imaginary friend. "Anything bad I did, I blamed it on Booey, the evil twin I created when I was a little boy."

Jessica Biel as Mary Camden

Although *7th Heaven* marked her television debut, Jessica Biel was no stranger to the camera. Jessie, as her friends call her, spent two years doing print and commercial modeling prior to landing her role on the show.

Growing Up Jessie

Born on March 3, 1982, in Ely, Minnesota, Jessica spent her early childhood moving from city to city, home to home, and school to school. She's lived in Texas, Florida, Connecticut, and Colorado. Wherever she went, Jessica had little trouble fitting right in. Aside from being obviously pretty and vivacious, Jessica made lots of friends through playing sports.

Always looking for an outlet for her boundless energy, Jessica took an interest in singing and began voice lessons at the age of eight. But, a young actress was about to emerge. As Jessica recalled in *Teen Beat*, "I started auditioning for different plays and little theater things at school and summer camp. When we moved out to Colorado, I continued with singing." Jessica appeared in regional productions of *Annie, The Sound of Music, Beauty and the Beast, The Invisible People,* and *Anything Goes.*

Local commercials soon followed, but little did Jessica know she was "this close" to being discovered. "I got this agency in Colorado and they said, 'Why don't you come to the International Modeling and Talent Association with us?' so I went to California." After competing in singing, acting, and modeling competitions in front of judges, a well-known acting teacher stood up and took notice of Jessica. "The teacher's name was Diane Hardin and she gave out a scholarship every year to her acting school and I got that scholarship! I decided to come out and use that so I wouldn't have to pay for acting classes," Jessie explained.

Bright Lights, Big City

"When I told my parents I wanted to do this acting thing," Jessica told *YM,* "they said okay, so I was like, 'Yeah, let's go!'" So, in 1994 the family moved to California, where Jessie spent two years modeling for such fashion campaigns as Limited Too. In 1996 Jessica auditioned for *7th Heaven* and landed the part of Mary Camden, beating out many other hopefuls. As a fresh-faced teen high on life and in love with sports, Jessica was perfect for the role. In fact, of all the actors on *7th*

Heaven, Jessica is, without question, the most like her character.

"It's really funny because I'm a lot like her. It's exactly who I am," Jessica confessed to *16* upon landing the role. "She's a very strong person, very independent, but very cool. Mary's very athletic, too, and I love to play sports. We're just so much alike it's kind of hard to think of something that's different about us."

A newscaster at the WB asked Jessica what she thought of *7th Heaven* and her response was over the top. "Our shows are awesome, our writing is great, and our cast is wonderful. I mean, just everything with the show is just so much fun. I'm having a great time."

That "great time" follows Jessica off the set, too, where she's been known to play almost every sport. "I love to play football, basketball, and hockey," she told *Tiger Beat.* "And I play soccer and gymnastics and swimming and every other sport there is." There's more to Jessica than acting and sports, though. For one thing, she plans to go to college, and not just part-time, she told *TV Guide.* "If I'm gonna go, I gotta go. It can't be like, 'There's this audition, should I do it, should I not?'"

Being Successful Means Being Busy

Indeed, Jessica's future looks bright. In addition to *7th Heaven*, Jessica's professional life has included two movies, *It's a Digital World* and the critically acclaimed *Ulee's Gold*, in which she played Peter Fonda's rebellious granddaughter. Jessica won a Young Artist Award for her work in the film. She's also found time for photo shoots with *Sassy, YM*, and *Seventeen*.

During the show's second summer hiatus, Jessica joined another TV teen, *Home Improvement* heartthrob Jonathan Taylor Thomas, in the movie *I'll Be Home for Christmas*. "She's a very good actress," Jon told *Teen Beat*. "She's very funny and a nice person to be around." Jessica plays the ex-girlfriend of Jonathan. He spends most of the movie trying to win her back. The romantic comedy was filmed on location in Vancouver and Alberta, Canada, as well as in California. Of course, Jessica's no stranger to traveling.

Still the Same Ol' Jessie

No matter how busy Jessica gets, she always finds time for her two favorite people, her little brother Justin and her best friend Jesse. "I've never had a friend like Jessica," Jesse told YM. "Jessica is someone I can be crazy with and also someone I can tell everything to. We can be as wild or as dorky as we want, but our opinion of each other never changes."

Has success changed Jessica? Not according to her *I'll Be Home for Christmas* co-star, Jonathan Taylor Thomas. "She's really unaffected by this business and very down-to-earth," he told *Teen Beat*. Want to know what Jessica did with her very first paycheck? She hid one thousand dollars for her brother to find in a treasure hunt so he could buy himself a stereo he really wanted. Now, *that's* a big sister.

Jessica has a word of advice for some young actors. "Have fun with it and when you go on auditions, don't say to yourself, 'I have to get this thing.' If you get it, that's great, but if you don't, it wasn't meant to be, so there's something else for you later. You just have to wait your turn."

Just Jessie

NAME: Jessica Biel

DATE OF BIRTH: March 3, 1982

HOMETOWN: Born in Eli, Minnesota Raised in Danbury, Connecticut, and Boulder, Colorado

HEIGHT: 5' 7"

HAIR: Light brown

EYES: Green

SIBLINGS: Younger brother Justin

HOBBIES: Singing, dancing, soccer, and in-line skating

FUN FACTOID: Getting a driver's license was more of a challenge for Jessica than becoming an actress. As she explained in *TV Guide,* "I had no time to do driver's ed, and my parents were stuck on me doing it. I was so bummed about it." When she got her permit, Jessica practiced with her mom and dad in the studio parking lot. She had one mishap — she crashed the family car into a trailer!

David Gallagher as Simon Camden

Is there anyone in the world as adorable as *7th Heaven*'s Simon Camden? He's sweet, playful, and too cute for words, yet he knows exactly what he wants and is determined to get it. David described his character in an interview with *Teen Beat*: "Simon is very single-minded and if he doesn't get what he wants, he just doesn't give up. When Simon wanted a dog, he kept bugging his parents — bugging, bugging, bugging — until his mom finally went to the pound and came back with this really cute terrier." Of course, Simon is also the first Camden kid to run to Mom with a hug, or brighten a sad sibling's day with his precious smile.

Two Peas in a Pod

Believe it or not, David Gallagher is a lot like that in real life. Anyone who's ever met him will tell you he's even cuter, sweeter, and more playful in person. As for knowing exactly what he wants, ask David what his favorite food is, as an unsuspecting reporter did, and you won't believe your answer. "My favorite dinner is steak with mashed potatoes with my dad's gravy, corn on the cob, Stove Top stuffing, and butter noodles. It's so good!" *That's* a boy who knows *exactly* what he wants.

The similarities between David and Simon don't end there. Like Simon, David has four siblings — two sisters, Michelle and Kelly, and two brothers, Kyle and Killian — but in real life, he is the oldest. David's siblings also double as his best friends. "Since we live at the end of a long, twisting road in the middle of two mountains, there aren't a lot of kids around, so I have to make do with my brothers and sisters." David also finds company with his dog, Nomad. "He's a Rotweiller," David told *Teen Beat*. "When people hear that, they're usually like, 'Uh-oh,' but I think of him as a big, fat teddy bear because all he does is walk around the house and wants to be petted and loved and hugged."

David and his character are almost exactly alike "except that the family in *7th Heaven* is a little too nice to each other," David described. "Other than that, they are pretty much alike." In real life, he says, "We're a regular family with traditions and everything. For Christmas, we always do the tree together."

Recess

What does David do in his free time? "Four things — read (he collects *Goosebumps*), play video games, watch TV (his favorite show is *ER*), or see a movie." He spends his allowance on "books, toys, and music," he confessed. "The clothes are my mom and dad's thing." David also watches cartoons, collects toys, listens to Metallica, and does homework (his favorite subject is science) and chores, like a regular kid. "My biggest chore is — my dad calls it an obligation — keeping my room straight." The life of a young actor isn't always so glamorous!

From the Top

Born on February 9, 1985, in College Point, New York, David began his acting career when he was just a baby. "When I was a year old, my mom answered an ad in the paper and took me to this open audition," he recalled. David hooked up with a manager there and from that point, the ball started rolling and hasn't stopped since. "I started in magazine and newspaper ads and then I went to diaper commercials, then bigger commercials, and then I went up to movies-of-the-week, then movies, and now I'm at my final step — a TV series."

Among the commercials David appeared in were ones for Disney, Hanes, Burger King, and Tyson Foods. The TV movies include *It Was Him or Us, Father's Day, Bermuda Triangle, A Dad's Life, Summer of Fear,* and, most recently, *Angels in the Endzone.* David also had a guest appearance on *Walker, Texas Ranger* and a recurring role on the since canceled soap opera, *Loving.* Additionally, David holds the distinction of having appeared in two movies with John Travolta. "He's the coolest guy," David told *Tiger Beat.* He first

Secret: David bites his nails and mumbles in his sleep.

played the son of John and Kirstie Alley in *Look Who's Talking Now* and then played Kyra Sedgwick's son in the very successful *Phenomenon*.

David has an exciting career and future as an actor. When asked if he plans to go college, David explained, "Yes, actually, I do. I want to study directing and editing. When I go to college, I don't want to major in English literature, I'd rather do theater and fine arts." Meanwhile, you can expect David to continue acting. "Most definitely. This is my life, this job."

"When I was eight years old I saw myself on the big screen for the first time (in *Look Who's Talking Now*). We were in the very first row. I was so excited at the end of the movie that when the lights came back on, I jumped up and turned around and yelled, 'Hey, everybody! How'd you like the movie?' And everybody went, 'Oh, my gosh!'"

David's Deal

NAME: David Gallagher

DATE OF BIRTH: February 9, 1985

HOMETOWN: Born and raised in College Point, New York

HEIGHT: 4' 7" — and growing

WEIGHT: 85 lbs.

HAIR: Blond

EYES: Green

SIBLINGS: 2 younger brothers, Kyle and Killian, and 2 younger sisters, Michelle and Kelly

PETS: A dog, Nomad

HOBBIES: Collecting toys, watching cartoons, listening to hard rock music, and reading Goosebumps books

Beverley Mitchell as Lucy Camden

One of the most interesting facts about the cast of *7th Heaven* is that the actress who plays middle sister Lucy, Beverley Mitchell, is actually a year older than the actress who plays eldest sister Mary, Jessica Biel. But, despite looking young for her age, Beverley Mitchell is a teenager wise beyond her years.

From Tantrums to Auditions

The honor student and cheerleader from southern California already had an impressive acting résumé by the time she was cast for *7th Heaven* at the age of 15. In fact, Beverley's professional career began when she was four years old. "I was throwing a tantrum in a mall," Beverley recalled in *Teen Beat*, "and a talent agent said, 'Hey, do you want to be in acting?' So, acting up in a mall

is not always bad. That's how I got my start." Beverley's very first job was an AT&T commercial.

Many other commercials followed, for products such as Cream of Wheat hot cereal, Iron Kids bread, Energizer batteries, and two for the Disney videos *Sleeping Beauty* and *Lady and the Tramp*. In Beverley's most memorable commercial role, for Oscar Mayer, she complained to the bakery man that the hot dog buns were too long for the hot dogs. The little girl in the hot dog commercial stuck in the minds of lots of people, notably the casting directors of *Days of Our Lives*, who made Beverley a guest star when she was seven.

A number of other guest appearances followed on TV shows like *Quantum Leap*, *Baywatch*, *Melrose Place*, *Big Brother Jake*, *Phenom*, and *The Faculty*. Beverley also popped up in several TV movies, including *White Dwarf* and the miniseries *Sinatra*. She starred as Jersey in a series of TV movies

entitled *Mother of the Bride*, *Baby of the Bride*, and *Children of the Bride*. *Beverley* has also been in two feature films, *The Crow: City of Angels* and *A Killing Obsession*.

The Real-Life Beverley

It all began for Beverley Mitchell on January 22, 1981, in Pasadena, California. Born and raised there, Beverley had an all-American upbringing that included horseback riding, cheerleading, family road trips, and lots of pets. As a kid, she had two dogs and a cat. "Now I have Tigger, and he's 30 pounds. He's a fat cat," Beverley described. "I have Casper, too. He's a black cat."

In many ways, this typical California teen isn't unlike her *7th Heaven* character, except for one noticeable difference. "I've always been an only child and now I have lots of brothers and sisters," Beverley explained. "I cannot picture so many kids and one bathroom. That would be way too complicated," she kids. "It's interesting, I think it's really a lot of fun."

Otherwise, Beverley and Lucy are very similar. "I think I'm like my character," she said in *Teen*. "She's sensitive, she doesn't want people to be mad at her, and she really cares about others. I think Lucy's very sensitive and loving, and I'm just like that." She sure is. In fact, after filming the pilot episode for *7th Heaven*, Beverley bought gifts for everyone in the cast and crew.

"I like to go shopping, but I don't like to just blow money," Beverley revealed in *16*. "I like to buy presents for other people." She's also been known

to make crafts for her friends and co-stars, too. What other activities keep Beverley busy away from the *7th Heaven* set? "I'm a cheerleader. I like to horseback ride and I like to sing," she said. She also enjoys other sports like in-line skating, soccer, basketball, and swimming, as well as reading and, her number one pastime, going to the movies.

"My favorite actress is Jodie Foster," Beverley told *Tiger Beat*. "She's so great." Both Beverley and Jodie Foster began their careers as child actors. And, like Jodie, Beverley is beginning to get recognition for her talent and hard work. In the spring of 1998, Beverley was honored with a Young Artist Award—Leading Young Actress—for Best Performance in a TV Drama Series. When a *Teen Beat* reporter asked Beverley where she will keep her Emmy Award if she ever wins one, she said, "I would put it somewhere so no one could get a fingerprint on it. Except I know my cat would get it."

"I don't really have one favorite actor, but I really like Jodie Foster, Winona Ryder, and Susan Sarandon. I also love Sean Connery. I think he's so masculine."

Ever Beverley

NAME: Beverley Mitchell

DATE OF BIRTH: January 22, 1981

HOMETOWN: Born and raised in Pasadena, California

HEIGHT: 5' 2"

WEIGHT: 98 lbs.

HAIR: Blond

EYES: Blue

SIBLINGS: None

PETS: Two cats, Tigger and Casper

FUN FACTOID: As part of a Zillions magazine report on peer pressure, Beverley offered up a valuable lesson she learned as a kid. "I did what I thought my friends liked. I tried to adapt myself to please them. Then I realized they liked me for me and I stopped pretending."

David's Birthday Party
— You're Invited!

Have you ever wondered what celebrities do to celebrate their birthdays? The truth is, young **TV** stars like David Gallagher have good, old-fashioned get-togethers. In fact, when David has a birthday party, he invites all of his friends and has cake and balloons, plays games, and opens cards and presents just like you do. If you want to see for yourself, come on along and join in all the fun and laughs — this was the scene at David's 13th birthday party.

With cameras flashing, the birthday boy hams it up!

David's *7th Heaven* co-star, Beverley Mitchell, drops in to help him celebrate.

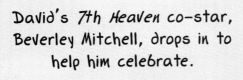

Later, Beverley discovers David's worst-kept secret — he's very ticklish!

A typical boy, David loves to wrestle with his pals. Hey, wait, that's *fudge* star Jake Richardson!

When a TV star has a party, a few celebrities are bound to show up. Here, David pals around with fellow actors Beverley, Jake, and Toran Caudell, an up-and-coming actor whom you may recognize from his recurring role on *Roseanne* or the Showtime movie *Max Is Missing*.

Of course, not all of David's friends are celebrities. Here he shows he's just an ordinary dude at heart, enjoying his birthday cake with some pals.

Beverley looks on in amazement at two huge birthday cakes. Hey, when a popular guy invites loads of friends to his party, there are a whole lot of hungry mouths to feed.

As David makes a wish and blows out the candles, Beverley begins to wonder if he'll need help.

Just as David is about to chow down on some cake (notice he opts for chocolate), he is joined by a swarm of friends and family.

Always the polite one, David puts his anticipation aside and opens the cards before the gifts. This one makes him smile.

Look at all those presents. David digs through tissue, bags and wrapping paper hoping to uncover everything he's wished for.

It looks like he got what he wanted. Judging from David's ear-to-ear grin, it's been his best birthday yet.

Although David is an actor, he doesn't always have to be the center of attention. His 13th birthday party was a perfect example of how he shares the spotlight. As you can tell by the smiles on all of his friends' faces, both famous and not, David wasn't the only one who had a great time at his birthday party.

Meet the Rest of the Cast
Stephen Collins as Reverend Eric Camden

Eric Camden, minister, husband, and father, has dedicated his life to helping others. An entire community, including his own family, has grown to count on his heroic response to calls in the middle of the night. Stephen Collins has shown similar dedication toward his acting career. One of Hollywood's busiest actors, Stephen, who was born in Des Moines, Iowa and raised in New York, has countless roles to his credit.

Before *7th Heaven*, TV viewers were long familiar with Stephen from his role as Teddy's (Sela Ward) love interest on the series *Sisters*, as well as from the shows *Tattingers*, *Working It Out*, and *Tales of the Gold Monkey*. Over the years, he's starred in dozens of miniseries, including *The Two Mrs. Grenvilles*, for which he earned an Emmy nomination. Stephen also played John F. Kennedy in *A Woman Named Jackie*. He's been in dozens of TV movies and feature films. His latest big

screener is *The First Wives Club.* The multitalented star is also a writer and director. Aside from directing an occasional epiosode of *7th Heaven,* he was at the helm for two regional plays. Stephen is also a budding author with two novels under his belt, *Double Exposure* and *Eye Contact.*

Upon winning and quickly accepting the part of Rev. Eric Camden, Stephen researched his role by speaking with ministers across the country. "They were all very relieved to hear that the part is being portrayed in a really simple way," he told reporters when *7th Heaven* first launched. "I think most of the ministers feel like really simple people doing very hard work. Most of them are raising families and dealing with family issues. That's one of the things that attracted me to the show, too."

Catherine Hicks as Mrs. Annie Camden

As mother, wife to a minister, and keeper of her huge home, Annie Camden must wear many hats. Likewise for Catherine Hicks, the talented and dynamic actress who plays her.

The Scottsdale, Arizona, native has an impressive acting résumé that includes a variety of roles in television, movies, and theater. *7th Heaven* marks Catherine's fourth starring role in a television series, following *Winnetka Road, Tucker's Witch,* and the once-popular daytime soap opera *Ryan's Hope.*

From 1976 to 1978, Catherine made a name for herself as Dr. Faith Coleridge on *Ryan's Hope.* Since then Catherine's had numerous guest appearances and recurring roles on TV shows, most recently, *Diagnosis Murder.* Catherine also starred in the mini-series *Valley of the Dolls,* as well as many TV movies, including *Marilyn: The Untold Story,* for which she received an Emmy nomination. Catherine has also appeared in over 15 movies.

Catherine graduated from Cornell University, where she studied theater and appeared in many regional productions. One of the roles that Catherine is most proud of was co-starring opposite Jack Lemmon in the Broadway world premiere of *Tribute.*

"I love to act and I'm very grateful I have a career," Catherine said at a WB press conference, "but I have a four-year-old daughter and I go to preschool and meet the normal moms. A lot of them are really smart and educated and I don't know how they do it. They spend their entire day and evening trying to make a quality life for their kids. They're really dedicated women and they're sharp and happy. So, you know, that's who I'm playing."

Mackenzie Rosman as Ruthie Camden

On *7th Heaven*, youngest sibling Ruthie is constantly clamoring for attention. In real life, her counterpart, Mackenzie Rosman — or Mack as she prefers to be called — gets all the attention she could ever want as a star of a prime-time TV series. Before landing her role on the show, Mack appeared in a number of national commercials for products like Hormel Chili and Tuffs Diapers. *7th Heaven* marks her series debut.

A Los Angeles native, Mack was born on December 28, 1989. Her younger brother Chandler, who recently auditioned for his first commercial, provides competition for Mack. "The way we argue drives my mom crazy," she told *16*. In her free time, Mack likes to dance, swim, and skate.

Happy the Dog — as Happy the Dog

The happiest day of young Simon Camden's life was when his parents allowed him to adopt a playful and lovable mutt that he appropriately named Happy. As for the dog, the happiest day in *her* life was when she was rescued from a California pound when she was just a year old. As luck would have it, Happy (also the pooch's name in real life) was taken in by Shawn Webber, who happens to be the trainer of other celebrity animals, including Murray, the *Mad About You* dog. After receiving the professional guidance of Boone's Animals for Hollywood, Happy learned all the tricks she needed to audition for *7th Heaven*.

"I can tell you as somebody who has worked with a dog before, which I did once in a series a long time ago, that this is a great dog," professed Stephen Collins. The 30-pound, white terrier mix was cast in the role by series creator Brenda Hampton. Although this marks Happy's first and only acting job, "She's kicking it by the trainer's pool fielding offers," her trainer told *TV Guide*.

Barry doesn't mind being in a tux — exactly! He really prefers more casual duds.

Barry smiled for the cameras at a Teen People party. His date is a girl named Laura.

Behind the Scenes

While the Camdens reside in the fictional town of Glen Oak, the actual house and church used in the show are in Altadena, California, in the San Fernando Valley. Most of the scenes in *7th Heaven* are filmed at the show's studio base in Santa Monica, California.

The lot consists of several trailers with security and ample parking for all of the cast (cast members old enough to drive get their own personalized parking spaces) and crew. The smaller trailers have dressing rooms and make-up stations for the actors, and the largest trailer is where the bulk of the filming takes place. When you walk inside, it looks like an airport hangar divided into different sections for each part of the house. Until you look up to the ceiling, which is cluttered with high-powered lights, at times it really seems like you're *in* the house.

That's a Wrap!

It sounds serious, and it is, but with a young cast, there's always time for fun. During breaks in filming, Barry, Jessica, Beverley, and David pal around like real-life siblings. "It's seriously like a family," Jessica told *Tiger Beat*. "We're always playing jokes. It is so funny what happens on our set, it's crazy." What's been the biggest practical joke of all? "One day Beverley and I got these ads for Midol and PMS and stuck them all over Barry's trailer. When we came in the next morning, our whole trailer was completely covered in toilet paper. It was so funny!"

Don't the young actors worry about getting in trouble for their antics? "No, everyone does it, even the crew!" Jessica explained. "They'll come around and you'll feel something and go, 'What is that?' You pull it out and it's a string with a spoon hanging off and you've been walking around the whole set like that. It's cool!"

He took the same girl to a Christmas bash.

Jessie strikes a pose at a gala Hollywood premiere.

She strikes another [!!]
backstage at an
awards presentation.

Jessie attends an event with
last year's TV boyfriend, Andrew
Keegan, who played Wilson.

Aside from the pranks and gags, the cast also breaks for lunch. "We all go for lunch together," Jessica told a **WB** newscaster. "It's usually me, David, Beverley, and if Andrew's [Keegan] around. We'll go to my trailer and we'll play video games, wrestle, listen to music, watch videos, and play Ping-Pong." Jessica, Beverley, and David also have to find time for schoolwork. Sometimes they'll work on assignments or study for tests, and when it gets really busy, they have tutors come on the set to instruct them.

Meanwhile, the rest of the cast keeps busy in their own ways. Barry's often on the phone with family and friends, Stephen and Catherine are usually either chatting or reading, and all three stay on top of things by talking with the crew. Meanwhile, little Mackenzie simply catches up on her beauty rest.

In real life, Jessie is as athletic
as her character, Mary.

Beverley takes to the slopes for
a teen ski trip.

SKI
LIFT

David poses with his mom at a press event for the WB network.

David and actor buddy Jake Richardson do the photo-op thing at the Slam Site Game debut in Burbank, California.

The fact that Jessie wears glasses is something David and Beverley know!

Jessie's mom, Kim, and her brother, Justin, are two of her biggest fans.

Web Sites: Get On-line for 7th Heaven Info

If you're looking for still more information about *7th Heaven* and its stars, look no further than the Internet. The World Wide Web is chock-full of sites devoted to the show. In fact, if you input "7th Heaven" as a key word, you'll get a listing of about a thousand (!) Web sites. However, a good portion of them are for a greeting card company, a party planner, and an airline promotion — so be sure and narrow your search to entertainment/television first.

Even after you've gotten an accurate listing of *7th Heaven* Web sites off a search engine (AOL's search, Yahoo, Excite, or Lycos) you'll still find dozens to choose from, including official, unofficial, and downright amateur. Here's a list of what we think are the most informative *7th Heaven* sites on the Net.

The Official *7th Heaven* Web Sites

• *Warner Bros. TV Network*

www.thewb.com

Show background, cast bios, photos and links to other WB shows like *Dawson's Creek* and *Buffy the Vampire Slayer.*

• *Warner Bros. Virtual Lot*

www.virtuallot.com

General information, chat rooms, interactive games, and links to other shows and Warner Bros. movies.

• *WB Local Affiliates*

www.wb17.com or www.wphltv.com (Philadelphia)

www.wb11.com (New York City)

www.krrt.com (San Antonio)

Press releases, publicity photos, programming, and critics' reviews. Links to sites on individual cast members.

Fan Mail

If you don't have Internet access, or if you just want to send your very best to the cast and crew of *7th Heaven*, mail your letters, cards, or biscuits for Happy to:

7th Heaven c/o The WB Television Network, 3701 Oak Street, Burbank, CA 91505

Who's Got Next

The second season of *7th Heaven* went out with a bang, as the finale was the highest-rated episode in the WB's history. Going into the third season, fans were left with lingering questions, namely, how would the Camden family dynamic change with Matt in college and the new babies on the way?

Series creator Brenda Hampton promises the show's title will not change to "8th Heaven," or "9th Heaven" for that matter. But adding a set of twins to the mix will definitely create some chaos! As the show progresses, parents Annie and Eric will prove, again and again, that they can tackle any obstacle that gets in their way. With their loving kids pitching in — Brenda says Lucy will likely do the baby-sitting so Mary can go out — the warmest couple in America can accomplish anything.

What's in Store for the Stars

Barry Watson, Jessica Biel, and David Gallagher all appear to be well on their way to becoming movie stars as well as TV stars. The early buzz on Barry's performance in *Killing Mrs. Tingle* has him joining the ranks of "it" boys Matt Damon and Leonardo DiCaprio. And Jessica's sure to sizzle in *I'll Be Home for Christmas*.

David's doing the direct-to-video thing, co-starring with Michelle Trachtenberg in *Richie Rich's Christmas Wish*. As for Beverley, the straight-A student is set on going to college. Maybe some day she'll write a script for a movie that her three on-screen siblings will star in. Who knows? Mackenzie might just be old enough to direct by then.